WACKY
WEDNESDAY

GEORGE
WASHINGTON

WACKY WEDNESDAY

By **Dr. Seuss***

*writing as
Theo. LeSieg

Illustrated by **George Booth**

BEGINNER BOOKS®   A Division of Random House, Inc.

TM & text copyright © by Dr. Seuss Enterprises, L.P. 1974, renewed 2002.
Illustrations copyright © 1974 by Random House, Inc.
Illustrations copyright renewed 2002 by George Booth.

www.randomhouse.com/kids
www.seussville.com

Educators and librarians, for a variety of teaching tools, visit us at
www.randomhouse.com/teachers

Library of Congress Cataloging-in-Publication Data
Seuss, Dr. Wacky Wednesday. "59."
SUMMARY: Drawings and verse point out the many things that are wrong one wacky Wednesday.
ISBN-10: 0-394-82912-3 (trade) — ISBN-10: 0-394-92912-8 (lib. bdg.)
ISBN-13: 978-0-394-82912-8 (trade) — ISBN-13: 978-0-394-92912-5 (lib. bdg.)
[1. Counting books. 2. Stories in rhyme.] I. Booth, George, illus. II. Title.
PZ8.3.G276Wac [Fic] 74-5520

Printed in the United States of America   64 63

It all began
with that shoe on the wall.
A shoe on a wall . . . ?
Shouldn't be there at all!

Then I
looked up.
And I said,
"Oh, MAN!"

And that's how
Wacky Wednesday
began.

I looked out
the window.
And I said,
"GEE!"

More things were wacky!
And I saw three.

I went
down the hall
and I said,
"HEY!"

Three
more things
were wacky today!

In the
bathroom,
MORE!

In the
bathroom,
FOUR!

I began to dress.
Then I said,
"WOW!"

Four MORE things
were wacky now!

I looked
in the kitchen.
I said,
"By cracky!
Five more things
are very wacky!"

I was late for school.
I started along.
And I saw that
six more things were wrong.

And then seven more!

And the Sutherland sisters!
They looked wacky, too.

They said,
"Nothing is wacky
around here but you!"

"But look!" I yelled.
"Eight things are wrong
here at school."

"Nothing is wrong,"
they said.
"Don't be a fool."

I ran into school.

I yelled to Miss Bass . . .

. . . "Look!
Nine things
are wacky
right here
in your class!"

"Nothing is wacky
here in my class!
Get out!
You're the wacky one!
OUT!"
said Miss Bass.

I went out
the school door.
Things were worse than before.
I couldn't believe it.
Ten wacky things more!

Then I
counted
ELEVEN!

Then . . .
twelve WORSE things!
I got scared.
And I ran.

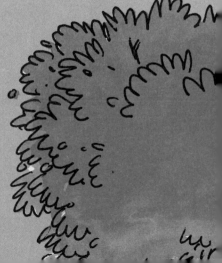

I ran
and knocked over
Patrolman McGann.

"I'm sorry, Patrolman."

That's all I could say.

"Don't be sorry," he smiled.
"It's that kind of a day.
But be glad!
Wacky Wednesday
will soon go away!"

"Only twenty things more
will be wacky," he said.

"Just find them
and then
you can go
back to bed."

Wacky Wednesday was gone
when I counted them all.
And I even got rid
of that shoe on the wall.

THEO. LESIEG and Dr. Seuss have led almost mystically parallel lives. Born at the same time in Springfield, Mass., they attended Dartmouth, Oxford, and the Sorbonne together, and, in the army, served overseas in the same division. When Mr. LeSieg, inevitably, decided to write a children's book, he was, happily, able to prevail on his old friend Dr. Seuss to help him find a publisher. Since then his stories have delighted millions of children around the world.

GEORGE BOOTH, whose drawings appear in many places (but most often in *The New Yorker*), has emerged as one of America's most admired and original cartoonists. Born in Cainsville, Mo., Mr. Booth got his start in the Marine Corps drawing funny pictures for *The Leatherneck*. He was art director with Bill Communications, Inc., for several years, then he threw a fit and returned to cartooning. We're glad he did.